Welcome to ALDAFIA

A Secret Land in Your Garden.

This magical book belongs to:

....

We fairies all agree,
that the special child who signs
this book can be free,
to explore ALDAFIA with Betty and Billy
and be as teeny tiny as a bee!

You must though make a promise
that forever you will keep,
that you will always believe in magic and
dream of fairies in your sleep!

Welcome to ALDAFIA
A Secret Land in Your Garden
(Based on a true story)

Phillip Boyd

For my children,
Thank you for the magic.
Daddy

KDP ISBN: 9798649870306

CONTENTS

A Secret Land in Your Garden.

One sunny day Mummy, Daddy, Betty and Billy went into the
garden to play.
For hours they ran and they wiggled,
they jumped and they giggled!
Later Mummy and Daddy went inside for a well-earned rest,
Betty turned to Billy and pointed North-West.
"Shall we draw a castle for a butterfly nest?"
Billy replied excitedly, "What a great way to play,
shall we draw another castle where the hedgehogs can stay?"

Slowly they added to their secret garden map,
inventing a land whilst Daddy had a nap!
Using their imagination and all the creatures under the sun,
they drew pictures of their characters and named every last one.
Adding a Fairy Hotel tree then a Bogey Goblin in the middle,
they created a magical land little by little!

But something was about to happen that no one expected,
the fairies said hello and real life was detected.
While the grown-ups were inside,
this new world had come alive!
Amazed, Betty and Billy stared at each other and had an
idea, "This is our secret land so let's call it ALDAFIA!"

With the sun slowly setting The Fairy Hotel lights turned on,
the characters started dancing and the magic was strong!
This is a place that no grown-up can enter,
but you'll find fairies, butterfly Queens and hedgehog Kings,
smiling spiders and lots more wondrous things,
all around its fairy tree centre.

With magic, laughter and excitement aplenty,
The Fairy Hotel was opened with rooms, one hundred and twenty.
It's run by the fairies;
Daisy, Bluebell, Lightning and Flower,
and let's not forget Strawberry,
who has great singing power!
They enjoy collecting sea shells and dancing with their guests.
We all love them and think they're the best!

Close to the stars and way up high in the tree,
live Leslie the Ladybird and Bernie the Bee.
One with red wings and sixteen black spots,
one with a stinger that could hurt lots and lots.
Another thing you should know about this couple up above,
is that they're completely and deeply in love.

They've been a family for years and get better with age,
can you find their little ones,
Lady Bee and Bumble Bird hidden on each page?
John the pigeon sits close by eating non-stop,
everyone is worried that one day he'll pop!

The pond in the south is filled with tadpoles and frogs,
where Trudy and Felicity love leaping over logs.
But unless you look closely you will not see,
it is the froglets that rule under the lily pad sea.
Their leader is Arnold and a warrior is he,
but it's best not to tell him he's the size of a pea!

Next to the pond is a cottage filled with big cobweb lines,
underneath them are snail trails that go on for hundreds of miles.
Our spiders are friendly and smiley it's true,
their best friends are the snails who are faster than you!
So welcome to Lloyd the smiliest spider and
Howard the slimiest snail,
friends forever until they are frail!

Not everyone is friendly as Betty and Billy will tell you. Crocs the
cat is a rascal, so shoo him away before he starts to wander.
If you don't, he will likely leave,
hidden for you in the spikey bush weave,
a small smelly number!
The birds are quite fabulous that is also true.
Their feathers are beautifully pink so meet Doreen our dearest,
she flies way up high and is totally fearless!

With The Fairy Hotel in the north and the froglets in the south,
we did not mention the royalty by mouth.
You remember the castles that were drawn with chalk?
Two kingdoms were born and their leaders can talk!
The Hedgehog King Spikes rules to the east,
whilst the Butterfly Queen Olivia has her nest in the west.

Both have great powers but did not dare step outside,
I bet you are wondering why they would hide?
Well we forgot to introduce you to the meanest of all,
the one they all fear and leave well alone.
The last on our list is the one with no manners, the one who picks
his nose and eats it, which is oh so disgusting,
but sometimes bizarrely he actually just keeps it!
He is the Bogey Goblin.

If the rumours are true, if he manages to touch you,
you will turn into a bogey.
He will then eat you or keep you and that is no jokey!
But until then we'll have fun and no hassle,
because we all play a running game called 'Castle to Castle'!

So now you know who lives in our garden and how ALDAFIA was created.

Maybe this could be your garden and a world will be born that will leave you elated!

Magic is in all of us, not only in this story,

your imagination is key to discovering its glory.

So, **"Welcome to ALDAFIA..."**

A Secret Land in Your Garden.

We've only just begun our magical journey and we'll have more adventures with heart.

This world is yours to create so imagine big things, go outside and make a start...

How to play 'Castle to Castle': A beginner's guide.

With some chalk draw a castle on one side of your garden.
If you don't have a fence plain paper will do,
either way make two ends so you can play in the middle bit too.

A castle at both ends for the King and the Queen.
In the middle the Bogey Goblin will stand looking mean!

You're only safe if you're stood in your royal plot.
If the Bogey Goblin catches you, you'll be stuck in green snot!
Run from castle to castle and have lots of fun.
But try not to get caught or your game will be done!

As you change into a bogey you will get really sticky.
You won't be able to move until a friend saves you quickly!

Be fast and be clever,
and remember you'll play better together!
Good luck to all.
Play safe and don't fall!

Welcome to ALDAFIN

The Fairy Hotel

The Fairy Hotel and the Grumpy Caterpillar.

The Fairy Hotel and the Grumpy Caterpillar.

If you struggle to remember ALDAFIA we will try to remind you,
but do not say it out loud as no grown up can know,
that this is a place where they cannot go.
It's a secret land hidden away,
where fairies and magical creatures dance and play.

This story starts at The Fairy Hotel which has rooms aplenty,
to be exact it has one hundred and twenty.
Small, bright and charming it says on the guide,
its rooms are connected by the world's longest slide!
A magical rainbow slide with one special thing you must know,
you can slide from the bottom to the top and it's definitely not slow!

You know who runs it by now,
but in case you forgot here's the know-how.
There's Daisy, Bluebell, Lightning and Flower,
and let's not forget Strawberry, who loves singing hour!

On this day in question a guest arrived who had a grumpy request.
A caterpillar named George walked up to the fairies and said quite sternly,
"I want one room way up high and it best not be dirty."
Strawberry replied politely, "Sir, all of our rooms are lovely and clean,
but please remember there's no need to be mean."
Looking angry and flustered, the caterpillar muttered,
"Just make sure it's spacious and send up some banana custard."
The fairies could see that there was no pleasing this guest
and they all thought it odd that he made such a strange request.

Up to his room he wormed and he wiggled with no
belongings at all,
in his bed he stayed with room service his only one call.
He spoke to the fairies demanding custard be sent
every ten minutes,
clear to all that his belly knew no limits!

As the caterpillar shouted, "More custard, right now",
Lightning and Flower looked shocked and raised an eyebrow.
Bluebell and Daisy both said with dismay,
"How can he eat so much custard and treat us this way?"

George the caterpillar chose to ignore them.
Holding his belly he burped quite foully,
slamming his door with a bang that shook the room loudly.

Hours went by and George did not make a tune,
his window was open and he had hidden in a
strange sort of cocoon.
A cocoon made of silk it transpired to be,
but what was happening underneath, nobody could see.

For hours then days he was hidden away,
the fairies began to suspect foul play.
Then one bright sunny morning something magical took place,
the silk cocoon split open and they could see a butterfly face!

Spreading its bright and colourful wings a voice that
sounded like George suddenly said,
"I want to say sorry for being so grumpy,
I felt so tired and my stomach was lumpy.
I knew I was changing and I was unprepared,
I felt angry and in truth I was actually scared.
I was so hungry that I forgot to be polite,
you must be upset and I bet I gave you all a fright."

"I left my house feeling unwell,
I didn't even tell my mummy who must be quite worried as well.
Please accept my apologies and consider this offer.
Come to my house and I'll bake a real big show stopper!"

The fairies looked puzzled then smiled at long last,
"Don't be silly my friend your grumpiness is in the past.
Changes are hard especially when you are young,
but you have said sorry and now it is all done".

Strawberry smiled and continued,
"We accept your apology and your kind invitation,
but where is your home so we can see your creation?"

George the Butterfly flew up into the air and explained as he pointed west,
"Look over there and you will soon see,
Queen Olivia is my mummy and I have the castle door key!

I could make you my favourite but I bet you can't guess
what it is?
It's a butterfly tradition made with a very modern twist!"
The fairies and George all laughed loudly, for it was only then
they all knew,
that George was not only a butterfly prince,
but he loved banana custard too!

The Bogey Goblin and the Brave Hedgehog Princess.

The Bogey Goblin and the Brave Hedgehog Princess.

You remember the castles that we drew in ALDAFIA with chalk?
Two magical kingdoms were born and their leaders could talk!

The Hedgehog King Spikes rules to the east,
whilst the Butterfly Queen Olivia has her nest in the west.
Both have great powers but did not dare step outside,
I bet you are wondering why they would hide?

We introduced you to the meanest and greenest of all,
the one they all fear and leave well alone.
The one with no manners who picks his nose and eats it,
but sometimes bizarrely he actually just keeps it!
He is the Bogey Goblin.

One bright sunny morning the little hedgehog Princess Ellie,
decided to go for a walk in her favourite pink wellies.
She longed to be a brave explorer one day,
declaring, "I will leave the castle for adventure and play."

She went to see her Daddy as permission she needed,
but he could not be found so with her mummy she pleaded,
"Queen Mummy, today is filled with splendid sunshine far and wide.
Can I take a brave explorer's walk and look for adventure outside?"

The Hedgehog Queen gave a concerned look.
"You know the worry that we all share,
the Bogey Goblin may give you a scare.
If the rumours are true, if he manages to touch you, you will turn into a bogey.
He will then eat you or keep you and that is no jokey!"

The little hedgehog princess looked puzzled and said,
"But will he really want to eat me up when I have spikes on my head?
Surely he would prefer ice cream and jelly instead!"
Her mummy smiled but added,
"I'm sorry my dear but no going outside,
I don't want to risk you being seen and ending up in his insides."

The little hedgehog princess next met her Daddy and said,
"King Daddy, today is filled with splendid sunshine far and wide.
Can I take a brave explorer's walk and look for adventure
outside?"
King Spikes replied, "Don't be silly sweet little hoglet of mine,
the Bogey Goblin will cover you with green nostril slime!"

The little hedgehog princess looked more puzzled than before,
"But why would he do that when it would make his nose really
sore?"
King Spikes replied firmly, "We were told he has done this before
but I do not know why,

he just looks really scary so I ordered no one walks by."
The little princess wasn't happy with the answers she was given,
so she rolled quickly under the castle drawbridge because she was
so very driven.
"The Bogey Goblin cannot be real as no one could be so mean,
I want to be a brave explorer so outside I will go to see if he can
be seen."

The little hedgehog princess tiptoed through the grass,
when she saw something that made her feel like she was about to
pass!

The Bogey Goblin stood up and looked scary and agitated,
he moved closer and closer but then looked sad and actually quite deflated.
Frightened, the hedgehog princess took two steps back quickly on the trot,
nervously she shouted, "Please don't eat me up or turn me into snot."

The Bogey Goblin stopped and suddenly began to get upset.
"Everyone is scared of me and I just don't know why,
I just want a friend to play with but instead they run away and
make me cry."

The little hedgehog princess reached out her hand and said,
"It's clear to me they are mistaken and I'll stop this rumour right away.
Let's have fun together, is there a game that you love to play?"

In reply the shy green little guy smiled and said,
"My favourite game to play when there is splendid sunshine far and wide,
is to take a brave explorer's walk and look for adventure outside."
It was as if they were both destined to meet,
for Ellie had now found a friend who also loved exploring on his tiny little feet.

Ellie said, "I was told that you turned everyone to snot,
but now I know that's not true, not one little jot.
They said you were unfriendly and actually very mean,
you can't be a Bogey Goblin because your nose is very clean!"
He grinned and replied, "I'm not a Bogey Goblin, I'm a Brian!
And I have to say you're as brave as a lion!"

Ellie the princess hedgehog and Brian the Friendly Goblin played for years to come,
best friends they became and they never again felt glum!
The lesson here is that looks can be deceiving,
what matters most is that you are friendly and receiving.
Treat people kindly, ask their name and get to know them,
the reward will be a friendship that is forever and totally awesome!

*We'll be back soon for more magical adventures in **ALDAFIA!***

COMING SOON!

Welcome to ALDAFIA - The Magical Rainbow Slide and a teeny tiny BIG ADVENTURE!

...Betty and Billy looked concerned and replied,
"We'd love to help but we're far too big to even get through the door,
we'd need to be teeny tiny to help you all more."
Bluebell and Daisy, Flower, Lightning and Strawberry suddenly flew in a circle and sang out loud,
"We Fairies all agree that Betty and Billy can be free,
to walk around ALDAFIA and be as small as can be."
Suddenly sparks and lightning whirled all around them and would you believe it,
they shrunk down in size and were no bigger than a blue tit!

For the first time ever, Betty and Billy could finally see,
The Fairy Hotel from inside the tree!
Stepping through the brilliantly bright and beautiful front door,
the hotel was much bigger on the inside that was for sure!

The fairies pointed to a golden reception desk,
right next to it was a space where the magical rainbow slide used to rest.
Lightning said, "One minute the guests were sliding up and down from their room,
its shining rainbow colours moving guests with a zoom!"
Bluebell continued, "The next minute it disappeared. It was gone.
We could not believe it because without it the guests would move on."

Where did it go? No one knew.
How could someone take a slide without leaving a single clue?
Betty and Billy stepped up to the plate,
"We will help you and begin to investigate!"

To be continued...

Printed in Great Britain
by Amazon